# RUBY'S CHINESE NEW YEAR

# RUBY'S CHINESE NEW YEAR

Vickie Lee

illustrated by

Joey Chou

GODWINBOOKS

Henry Holt and Company ■ New York

Henry Holt and Company, *Publishers since 1866*
Henry Holt® is a registered trademark of Macmillan Publishing Group, LLC
175 Fifth Avenue, New York, New York 10010
mackids.com

Library of Congress Cataloging-in-Publication Data
Names: Lee, Vickie, author. | Chou, Joey, illustrator.
Title: Ruby's Chinese New Year / Vickie Lee ; Joey Chou.
Description: First edition. | New York : Henry Holt and Company, 2018. |
Summary: As Ruby travels to her grandmother's house to bring her a gift
for Chinese New Year, she is joined by all of the animals of the zodiac.
Includes the legend of the Chinese horoscope and instructions for crafts.
Identifiers: LCCN 2017004954 | ISBN 978-1-250-13338-0 (hardcover)
Subjects: | CYAC: Chinese New Year—Fiction. | Animals—Fiction. | Zodiac—Fiction.
Classification: LCC PZ7.1.L437 Rub 2018 | DDC [E]—dc23
LC record available at https://lccn.loc.gov/2017004954

Our books may be purchased in bulk for promotional, educational, or business use.
Please contact your local bookseller or the Macmillan Corporate and Premium Sales Department
at (800) 221-7945 ext. 5442 or by e-mail at MacmillanSpecialMarkets@macmillan.com.

First edition, 2018 / Designed by April Ward and Sophie Erb
The illustrations in this book were digitally painted in Adobe Photoshop.
Printed in China by RR Donnelley Asia Printing Solutions Ltd., Dongguan City, Guangdong Province

3  5  7  9  10  8  6  4  2

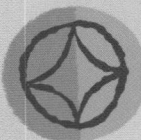

To my Nai Nai, Shu Jane Lee (李淑貞),
and to my Ruby Jane
—V. L.

For my mom, Julia, and all the
Chinese New Years we celebrated together
—J. C.

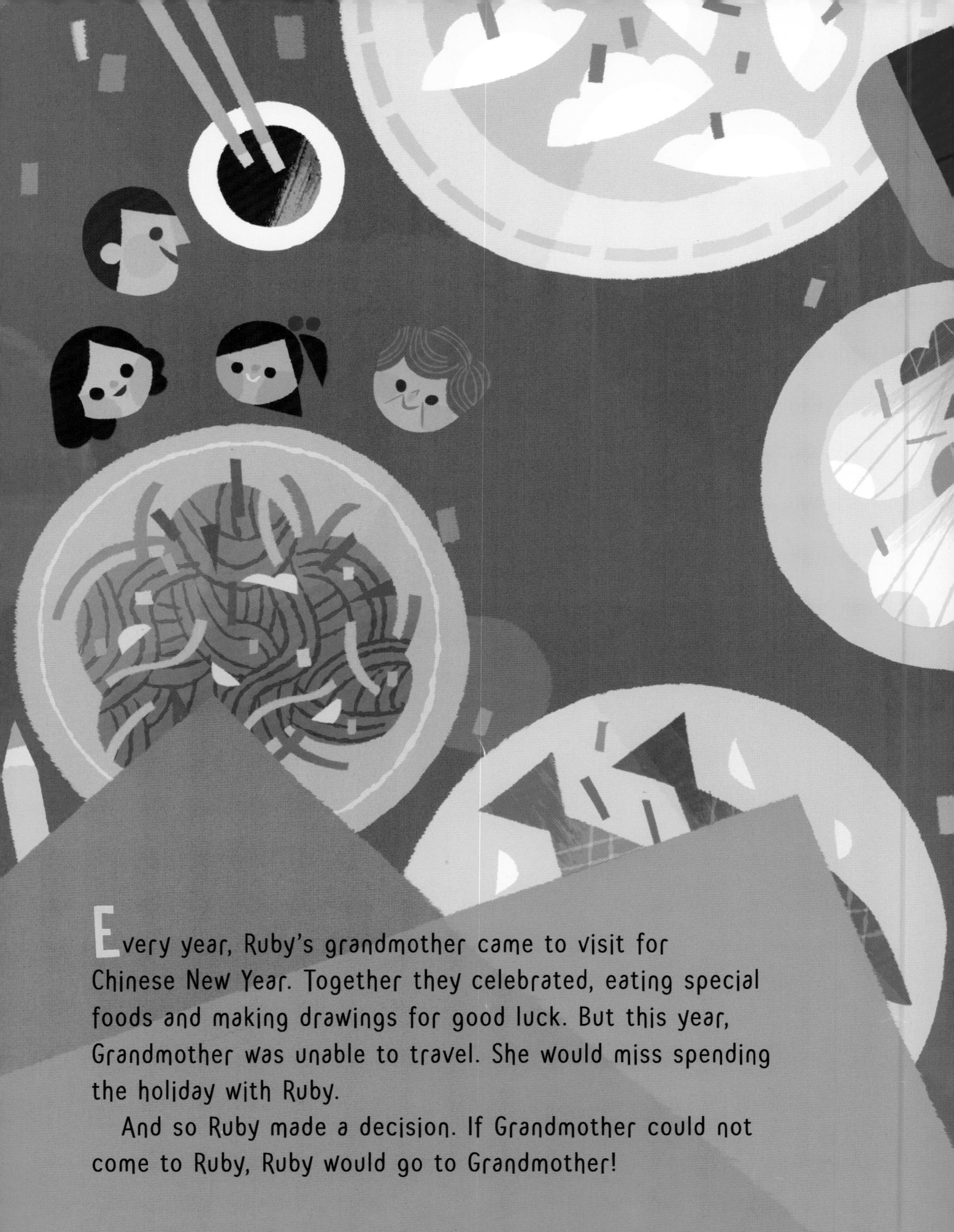

Every year, Ruby's grandmother came to visit for Chinese New Year. Together they celebrated, eating special foods and making drawings for good luck. But this year, Grandmother was unable to travel. She would miss spending the holiday with Ruby.

And so Ruby made a decision. If Grandmother could not come to Ruby, Ruby would go to Grandmother!

Ruby drew the most beautiful picture of her family seated around a table full of noodles, dumplings, fish, vegetables, and holiday sweets—a gift for Grandmother. She folded the red paper, tucked it into a red envelope, and slipped it into her pocket.

LOVE, RUBY

Then she set off!

Not far down the path, Ruby spied Cat and Rat.

"Hello, Cat and Rat. I'm taking a gift for Chinese New Year to Grandmother. Would you like to come along?"

"Yes, of course!" said Cat. "But how will we cross the meadow and the pond?"

"Let's ask Ox," said Rat. "She's so strong and dependable."

And so Cat and Rat and Ruby
continued on their way.

Ox was walking along the path to the farmer's home. On her back she carried packages of rice cakes and candies—sweet treats for the New Year.

"Hello, Ox," called Cat and Rat. "We are taking a gift for Chinese New Year to Grandmother. Would you like to come along?"

"I would be happy to," said Ox. "Climb on my back; we will make the journey together."

And so Ox, Cat and Rat, and Ruby continued on their way.

Before the group had taken two steps, Tiger and Rabbit
bounded out of the bushes, streamers flying behind them.
"Hello, Tiger. Hello, Rabbit," said Ox. "We are taking
a gift for Chinese New Year to Grandmother.
Would you like to come along?"

**"Oh yes, that
sounds fun!"**

said Tiger and
Rabbit in unison.

And so Cat took a seat on Tiger's powerful back, and Rat perched between Rabbit's soft, friendly ears.

Together, Tiger and Rabbit, Ox, Cat and Rat, and Ruby continued on their way.

They soon passed Dragon and Snake, who were making paper lanterns.

"Hello, friends! Where are you off to?" asked Snake.

"We are taking a gift to Grandmother," said Tiger. "Would you like to come along?"

"Of course I would!" Snake loved Grandmother and was happy to visit her.

"We will bring the lanterns," said Snake.
"Will you come too, Dragon?" asked Rabbit.
"Of course," said Dragon, who was always ready for an adventure.
So Dragon and Snake, Tiger and Rabbit, Ox, Cat and Rat, and Ruby continued on their way.

As they walked along,
Ruby saw Horse and
Goat grazing
in the meadow.

"Hello," said Dragon and Snake. "We are taking a gift to Grandmother. Would you like to come along?"

"Yes," said Horse and Goat together.

First they gathered flowers from the meadow. Then Horse and Goat, Dragon and Snake, Tiger and Rabbit, Ox, Cat and Rat, and Ruby continued on their way.

After a short while, Horse and Goat, Dragon and Snake, Tiger and Rabbit, Ox, Cat and Rat, and Ruby reached the pond, where Monkey and Rooster were catching fish for the holiday feast.

And through the shrubs, just on the other side, Ruby could see—

# Grandmother's house!

With a **leap** and a **bound**, Ruby **dove** into the **Pond**.

She would swim
to Grandmother's!
She was so close.

When Ruby finally reached the other side of the pond, Monkey and Rooster, Horse and Goat, Dragon and Snake, Tiger and Rabbit, Ox, and Cat and Rat were waiting with her card for Grandmother.

"Oh no," cried Ruby. "It's ruined. Everything is ruined!"

"It's not ruined!" crowed Rooster.

"We have **fish**," said Monkey.
"And **flowers**," said Horse and Goat.

"We have **lanterns**," said Dragon and Snake.
"And **streamers**," added Tiger and Rabbit.

"We have **rice cakes** and **sweets**," said Ox.

"And we have our **family**,"

said Cat and Rat, looking
toward the house.

As Monkey and Rooster, Horse and Goat,
Dragon and Snake, Tiger and Rabbit, Ox, Cat
and Rat, and Ruby turned to look, Dog and
Pig came racing out to greet them. They
covered Ruby's face with kisses and tickled
her until she shrieked with joy.
    The door opened . . .

. . . and Grandmother appeared.

"Ruby! What a wonderful surprise,"

said Grandmother.

"I brought you a gift for Chinese New Year,"
said Ruby, "but it's wet. And ruined!"

"Don't worry," said Grandmother. "It will dry.
And seeing you and your friends today is the
best gift of all."

Together, Dog and Pig, Monkey and Rooster, Horse and Goat, Dragon and Snake, Tiger and Rabbit, Ox, Rat, Ruby, and Grandmother laid out their table. Everyone was ready to celebrate Chinese New Year.

Except for Cat, who had fallen fast asleep.

# The Legend of the Chinese Zodiac

The Jade Emperor, ruler of all gods within Chinese mythology, hosted a great race across a wide and dangerous river to decide which twelve animals would win a place in the Chinese zodiac calendar. Cat and Rat were best friends and came up with a plan to ride Ox across the river together. As Ox swam slowly through the deep water, Rat suddenly jolted forward, knocking Cat into the river. It was too dangerous to turn back, and Cat was left behind. As Ox approached the finish line, Rat jumped off her back and claimed first place for himself. After Rat and Ox came Tiger, Rabbit, Dragon, Snake, Horse, Goat, Monkey, Rooster, Dog, and Pig to fill the remaining places in the zodiac calendar. Poor Cat finished the race last and was too late to claim a spot. This is why—to this day—cats hate water and are enemies of rats.

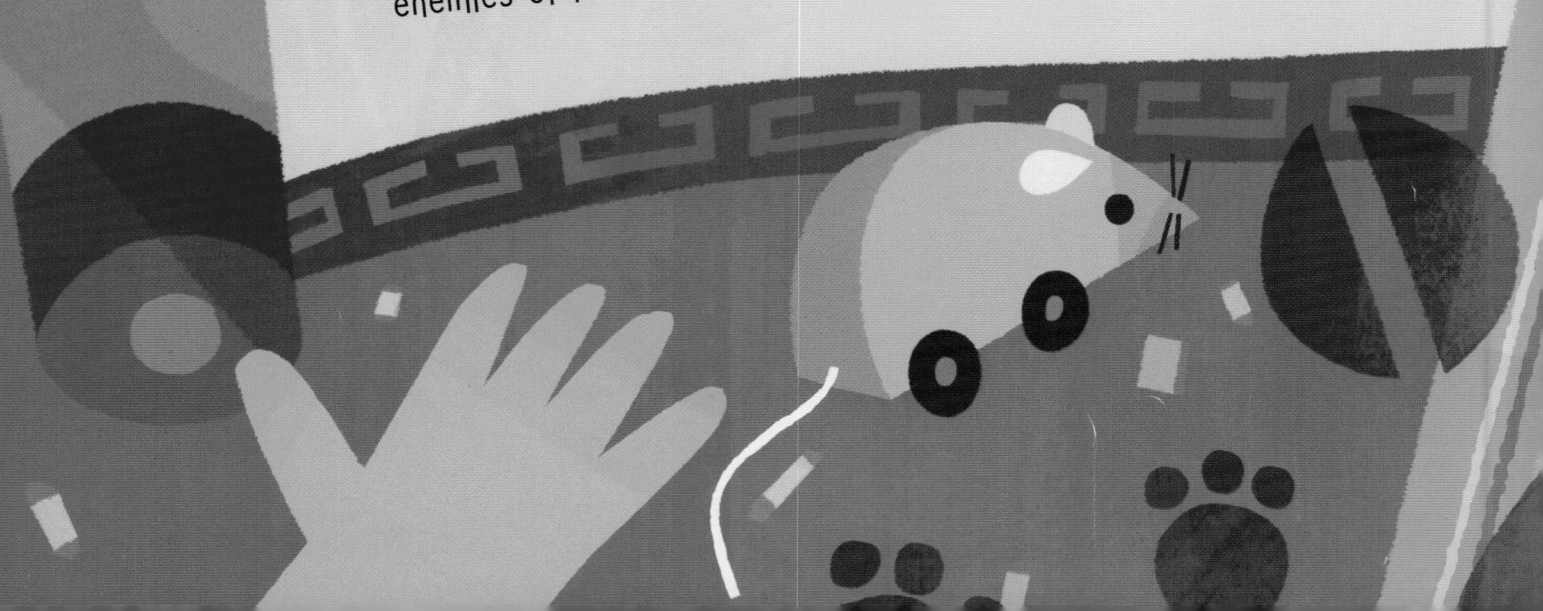

## RAT
2008, 1996, 1984, 1972, 1960
Clever, curious, loves to eat and stay up late, has talent for writing

## OX
2009, 1997, 1985, 1973, 1961
Hardworking, steady, trustworthy, loves to eat—especially snacks!

## TIGER
2010, 1998, 1986, 1974, 1962
Courageous, determined, a creative thinker, loves freedom

## RABBIT
2011, 1999, 1987, 1975, 1963
Friendly, even-tempered, quiet, peaceful

## DRAGON
2012, 2000, 1988, 1976, 1964
Independent, values equality, loves adventure, likes being the leader

## SNAKE
2013, 2001, 1989, 1977, 1965
Charming, sensitive, sociable, a careful planner

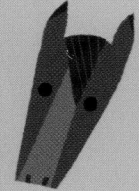

## HORSE
2014, 2002, 1990, 1978, 1966
Carefree, loves to travel and have fun, solves problems quickly

## GOAT
2015, 2003, 1991, 1979, 1967
Artistic, calm, kind, a good listener

## MONKEY
2016, 2004, 1992, 1980, 1968
...rt, entertaining, ...nerous, good with hands

## ROOSTER
2017, 2005, 1993, 1981, 1969
Witty, a great planner, has good judgment, loves colors and patterns

## DOG
2018, 2006, 1994, 1982, 1970
Honest, idealistic, loyal, responsible

## PIG
2019, 2007, 1995, 1983, 1971
Optimistic, caring, trusting, family-oriented, makes compromises

# CELEBRATE CHINESE NEW YEAR!

## MAKE A PAPER LANTERN

Traditional red lanterns are a fixture of Chinese New Year celebrations.

### Materials:

- Red construction paper
- Gold construction paper
- Pencil
- Ruler
- Scissors
- Glue

Step 1: Fold a sheet of red paper in half. Use the pencil and ruler to draw lines perpendicular to the folded edge, stopping one inch from the unfolded edge. Space lines about one inch apart.

Step 2: Use scissors to cut along the lines—these will form the slits of the lantern.

Step 3: Roll a sheet of gold paper to form a long tube, then glue the edges together. This will be the "light" at the lantern's center.

Step 4: Unfold the red paper and wrap it around the gold tube. Line up one edge with the bottom of the gold tube and glue.

Step 5: Glue the other edge of the red paper to the gold tube at the desired height. Cut off the excess gold paper poking out of the red lantern.

Step 6: Use a strip of gold paper to glue a handle to the lantern.

# MAKE A PAPER FAN

Fans have been used in China for centuries and make great decorations for Chinese New Year.

## Materials:

- Scissors
- Red construction paper
- Gold construction paper
- Glue
- Gold gift ribbon

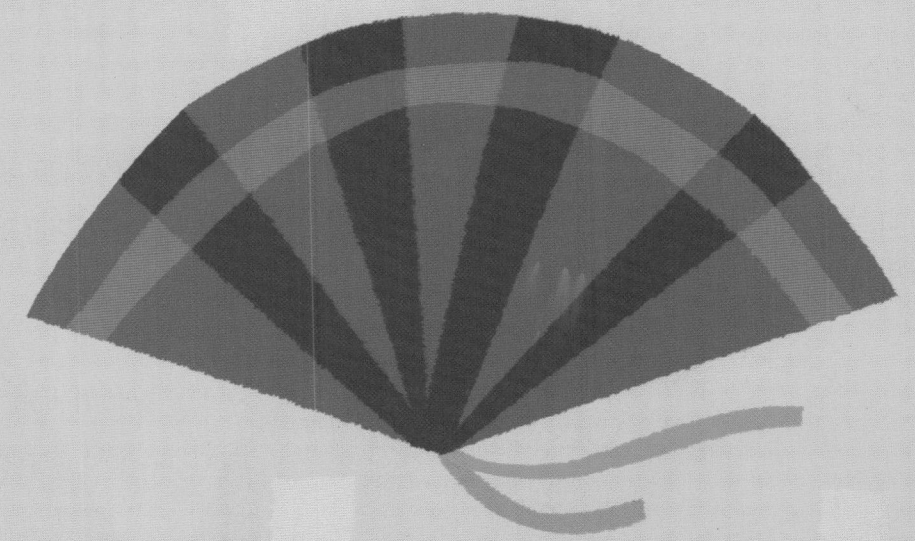

Step 1: Cut two thin strips of gold paper in a zigzag or other pattern. Glue the gold strips lengthwise onto a sheet of red paper, parallel to each other.

Step 2: Fold the paper back and forth to make pleats like an accordion.

Step 3: With the pleats still pressed together, fold the fan in half. Glue the two edges in the center together.

Step 4: At the bottom center, use the scissors to cut a small hole.

Step 5: Thread a length of gold ribbon through the hole and tie it to form a small loop with a tassel. This loop can be decorative or can be used to hang the fan.

# MAKE GOOD LUCK BANNERS

New Year, also known as the Spring Festival, is the longest and most important holiday in China. The festival is celebrated on the second new moon after the winter solstice, which often falls sometime between the end of January and the middle of February. It is a long-standing Chinese tradition to hang bright red banners and signs with messages of good luck for Chinese New Year.

## Materials:

- Red construction paper
- Gold construction paper
- Scissors
- Glue
- Red or gold ribbon
- Black or gold markers

**Step 1:** Cut the gold paper into a big square. Cut the red paper into a square an inch or so smaller than the gold one. Glue the red square onto the middle of the gold square.

**Step 2:** Cut a small hole in one of the corners. Thread a length of ribbon through the hole. Tie the ribbon in a bow or knot.

**Step 3:** Write a message of luck on your banner. Try copying the Chinese symbol above. It means "spring."